D0016883

RK
PRINCESS
SHARK PARTY!

NIDHI CHANANI
With color by
Elizabeth Kramer

VIKING

For Roberto,
who brings the party wherever he is

VIKING
An imprint of Penguin Random House LLC, New York

First published in the United States of America by Viking,
an imprint of Penguin Random House LLC, 2023

Visit us online at penguinrandomhouse.com.

Library of Congress Cataloging-in-Publication Data is available.

Manufactured in China

ISBN 9780593464649

1 3 5 7 9 10 8 6 4 2

TOPL

Text set in Nidhi Chanani
The illustrations were created created digitally with organic textures

Aloha! Today Mack and I are going to relax near my favorite coral.
But first, a snack!

SLUURRP

Whoa! That is a lot of krill! It's jawsome that you don't have to hunt your food.
crunch
crunch

Are you ready to go?
Where? I thought we were relaxing.

My food needs to settle. You *shouldn't* swim after you eat.

Aren't we **always** swimming?
Shore, and relaxing too.

Kitana! We're chums, and we're supposed to do things *together*.
I *love* doing things with you, Mack! What do you want to do?

Today is the SHARK PARTY!

I'm nervous about meeting a big group of sharks.

More sharks means more fun!

Oh, there's a warm current.

It's warm, but it's **not** a current.

Have you ever gone to a shark party?
No. Have you?

Nope! But I hear there are GAMES . . .

DANCING . . .

a feast . . . and of course LOTS OF SHARKS!

Don't you want to meet new sharks?
Not really.

I want you to come! It will be an adventure. Remember, *princesses love adventures*!
We *do* need a new adventure.

I guess we can swim by.
Swell!

Are you swimming to the party, too?
Yeah. How did you know? You're *not a shark*!

Yes, **I am!** I'm a *pancake* shark. We're cousins.
Oh!

Uh . . . what's a *pan-cake?*
You think it *means* something? Nah! Anyway, my name is **Raha.**

Party time!

Oh, I like your crowns!
Thanks! Are you a shark?
Shore am! Hammerhead shark.

Are you crownhead sharks?
No, I'm a mako shark, and she's a whale shark.
What's a ham-her head?

It's probably a made-up word like pancake.

I heard there will be a *feast*!
And dancing!
Look there!

Hello! Shark **roll call!**
Where's the feast?
Aloha!
Cookiecutter shark. What's a cookie?
I'm Tanay, a leopard shark.
Hi!
Looking at you makes me *sleepy*!
I'm a goblin shark.

I'm Fiza, a blue shark. But I'm *really* light gray.
Hey, dude!
I'm a nurse shark.
You all look the same to me.
Zebra shark here. I want a new name.
I forgot your names already.
Pyjama sharks here!
Anyfish heard of a carpet shark? That's me!

What's first?
Food!
Dancing?
Games!

It's a *party*! Let's do **all the things!**
Yeah!
Good idea.

shake
swirl
spin
shimmy
swoosh
zip

swirl
Kitana! Join us.
flip
zip
swoosh
shake

The water is *really* warm here.

Kitana? Where are you going?

All those sharks make me *shiver.* I need quiet.
Oh.

Fishnets! We didn't introduce ourselves as **SHARK PRINCESSES!**

Out of the wave!

Hey!
I need to share a **message.**
What message?

Swim and see.
Ohhh **yay!** We're going back to the party.

Hurry up, scallop!

Don't call my friend a *scallop*!
Do you know who we are?

It doesn't matter. I am **VANIN**, a great white shark. *The greatest.*
Oh yeah? We are shark princesses.

No fish is greater than a **PRINCESS.**
Do *you* have the message? Are *you* going to help?

We *will* help if we know the problem.

Friends, lend me your gills! A deep ocean shark was not invited to our party!

Oh.
And?
Uhh.

We should invite her!
It's *too deep*!
It's dark!
You can't see!
It's *cold*.

Why don't you go since you're so great?
I'm hungry.

Wait! I have an idea!

I'll use my SHARKLE!

Your what?!

My *shark sparkle!*
My **sharkle!**
Ohhh!
Ahhh!

I'm **Mack!**

I'm
Kitana!

We're *shark princesses*,
and we can help!

tail taps!

Holy mackerel! With your help, we can invite the deep ocean shark together.

Let's **go!**

uhhhh

Wait!
Can everyone spread out?

Uhh...

What now, *Princess?*

We're *too* many sharks!
Less is better.

Who should go?
Mack and I can go together.

We're *princesses*, and we **love** adventure.

Kitana, who are you smiling at?

Don't worry about it.
Oookay.

So you want to go . . . alone?
Are you scared, Mack?

Maybe?
Have you swam to the deep ocean?

No. Have you?
No, but I'm **ready** for another adventure! Our second adventure is *two-in-one*, double the fun.

We will invite the shark and return.

I didn't want to go anyway.
Did anyfish find food yet?
Let's go back to the party!
Why can't I sharkle?

This shark will be so *happy*!

Yeah, they're missing a **great** party!

It's so cold down here. Where's a warm current when you need one?

I can help with that.
You can?

No wave! You can warm water?! Is it your SPECIAL POWER, like my sharkle?
Yup.

No. Mack . . . Anyfish can . . .
Huh? Ohhhhhhhhh. KITANA! You pee a lot.

Princesses pee, too.

Who are you talking to down here?

Whoa.

We don't need my sharkle anymore.

Cooool.
Yeah.

Do you sense the shark yet?
Yeah, up ahead.

I feel its energy radiation.

Excuse us, are you a shark?
Yes.

We are here to invite you to a **shark party**!

Oh . . . thanks. But no thanks.

What? Don't you want to meet the other sharks?
I'm fine here.

Krill! We swam here for *nothing*!
Thanks for swimming down to invite me.

I'm **Adriana,** ninja lanternshark.
I never saw another shark
before. That's nice.

Never?
Nope.
But I like
being alone.

You do?
Yeah. It's calm down here. Want a tour?

Yes. Such pretty lights.

What's that smell?

Dead fish, probably.
Oh no!

Here it comes.
What's happening?

AH-AH
Mack is allergic to dead fish.

CHOOOOO
Oh my! Surface sharks are strange.

That was *loud*, excuse me.
He is **not** strange.

Mack's allergies *saved my life*!
Oh, wow. I didn't know. There's so much to learn about other sharks.

I'm so *comfortable* down here. I never thought about leaving and learning.

You can come visit us anytime.
Thanks! But I will take it slow. I already feel full of new information.

I'm glad you came, even though I don't want to party.

I'm going deeper to be alone. Thanks again!

You're welcome.

Now what?
We return to the party and tell them.

Right, the party.
C'mon.

I think I'm kind of like Adrina.

You are?
Yeah. I like being alone.

You do?
I like being with you, too!

Maybe I'm not like her exactly.

I'm like me! I like time alone, and I like being with you and our adventures.

I like being with you and our adventures, too!

Aloha, sharks! We invited Adrina, the ninja lanternshark.

She's nice but dislikes parties. Some sharks like to be alone, and that's okay.

And some sharks like to party, which is also okay!

Yay!
I love to party.
Is it time to feast?
I want to dance.

swirl
spin
shake
swoosh
zip
zip

If I spin fast enough, I can **sharkle!**
So *jawsome!*
That crown would look better on me.
Too bright! I wish I could close my eyes.
Do you want to dance?
Partying makes me hungry.
Nice moves!
I feel happy as a clam.
Does *your* crown sharkle?
Clams are *delicious!*
You look like you need fresh air.
This is **fintastic!**

What do you want to do?

Kitana?

I don't want to stay,
but you can.

What are you
going to do?
Swim home.

Can I join you after I eat?
Shore!

Mack, **wait!**

Changed your mind?
No . . . I wanted to warn you that you might be allergic to the feast.

You're right!
Bummer. I'm hungry.
grumble

You **saved** me, Kitana!
You're the *best chum.*
Want to swim
home together?
I'd love that!

Hold on, I need a mollusk snack first.

Feel better?

I always feel better after I eat.
Me too.
burp

Ready for relaxing?
Yes!

I can't wait for our next adventure!

The shark party and diving into the deep ocean weren't enough?

It was; I loved our double adventure! But . . .

What if we had THREE in one day? Thinking about it makes me excited!

Okay, but let's relax first.

Mack!

What? You're not the only fish that can make the water warm.

Relieving is relaxing!

THANKS for SWIMMING BY!

HIDE AND SEA

Can you find all of the sea creatures below in the pages of this book?

Deep Sea Anglerfish

Giant Isopod

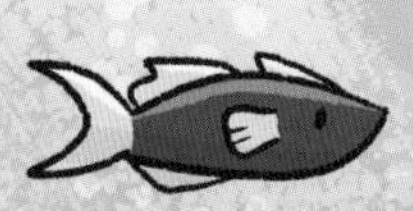

Blue Triggerfish

Wunderpus Octopus

Lion's Mane Jellyfish

Moorish Idol

Periwinkle Sea Snail

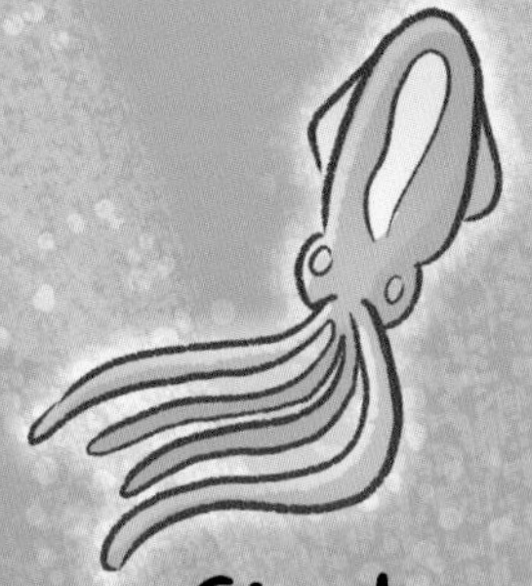

Giant Squid

Zebra Lionfish

SHARK FACTS:

MAKO SHARKS

One of 400 kinds of sharks!

SHARK PARTY

A group of sharks is called a shiver

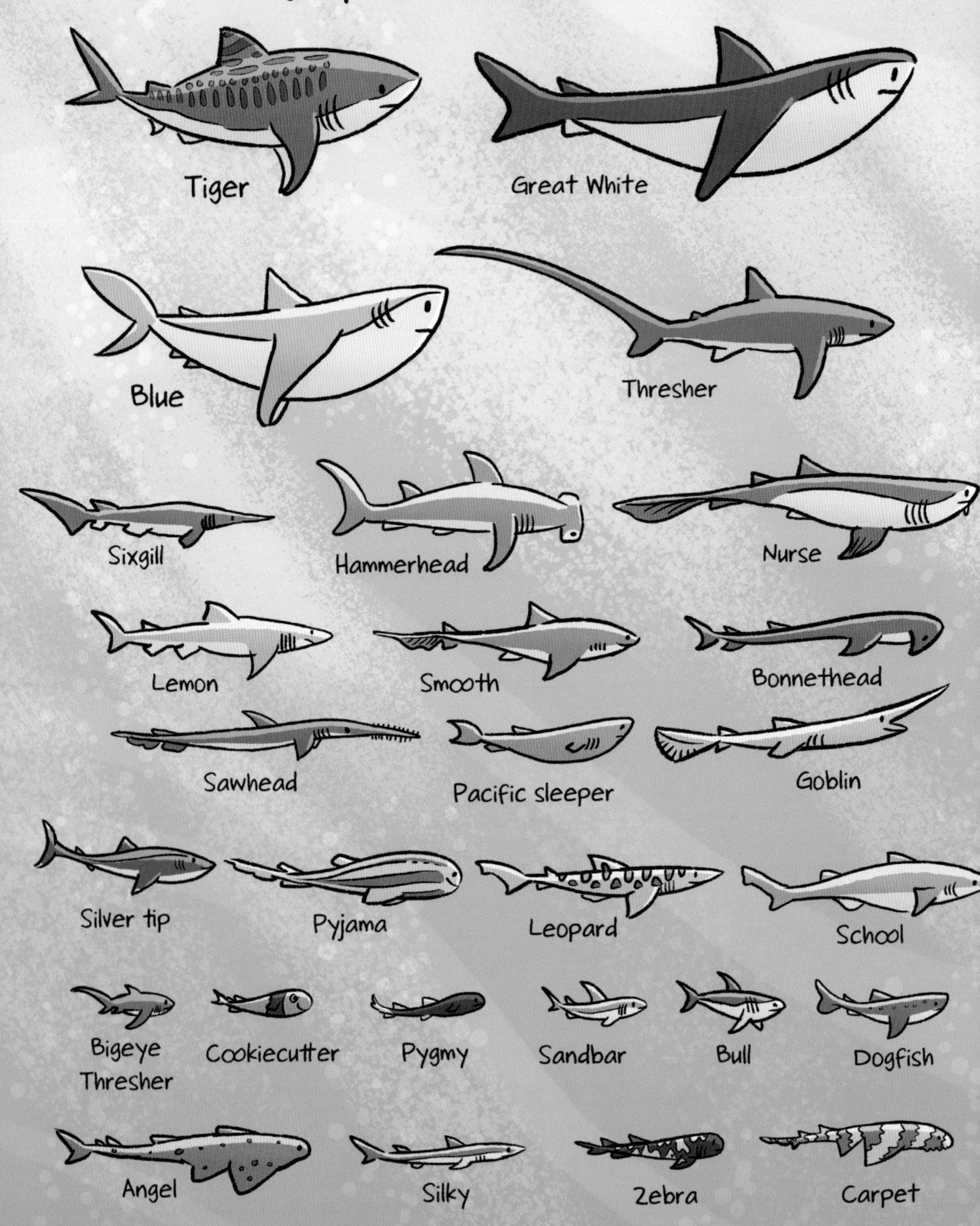

DRAW MACK

Learn how to draw the best chum in the ocean

Nidhi Chanani spends her days drawing and her nights dreaming of snorkeling. She's the author of the graphic novels *Pashmina* and *Jukebox* and the picture book *What Will My Story Be?* and the illustrator of many picture books, including *I Will Be Fierce*. Nidhi likes to party where she lives by the Pacific Ocean in the San Francisco Bay Area with her husband, daughter, and cats. Find more of her work at EveryDayLoveArt.com.